Millicent the Monster

by Mary Lystad

pictures by Victoria Chess

1st printing ....September 1975

Printed in the U.S.A.

SCHOLASTIC BOOK SERVICES
NEW YORK • TORONTO • LONDON • AUCKLAND • SYDNEY • TOKYO

On the day
that Millicent grew tired of being polite
—of saying "Please" and "Thank you"
and "Good morning, Aunt Emma"—
she decided to be a monster.

So she told
her little brother
she would eat him up.

And she told
the big boy across the street
that she'd hang him
from the highest tree.

Then she went
to her friend Sally's house and
—nose to nose, eye to eye—
she told Sally
that she would turn her purple all over.

She told her mother
that she didn't like her cooking…
and her father
that she was leaving home.
She was going far away
and she could do exactly as she pleased.
And what she pleased
was to eat people,
or hang them up in trees,
or at least turn them purple.

Millicent's mother was sad.
Her father was mad.
But her Aunt Emma
thought it was all very funny...

Until Millicent told Aunt Emma
she'd put her in a cage for laughing.

Millicent stomped outside,
crushing everything in her path.
She made faces at passing motorists.

She stood in people's way,
especially if they were grownups
and had big packages.

When Millicent was tired,
she skipped back home
and went into the good-smelling kitchen
and asked her mother
if she could have one of the still-warm cookies
on the cookie sheet.
But her mother told her
they were for the school bake sale.

She went to Sally's house
to see if Sally could play.
But Sally couldn't,
because her grandma was visiting.

But did Millicent care?
Of course not!
Or did she?...

Millicent went back to Sally's house and
—nose to nose, eye to eye—
she said she would not turn Sally
purple all over.

Then she went home to her mother
and said
that she really did think
her mother's cooking was delicious.

She went to her father and Aunt Emma
and said she wasn't a monster any more.
Her father sighed.
Her Aunt Emma played a song to celebrate.
And that was the end of that...